The Little Big Clockmaker

Written by

Evelyn Winters

A tale brought to you from the heart of Chester...

The Little Big Clockmaker
Copyright © 2015 by Evelyn Winters
Myths and legends for children

All Rights Reserved.
No Part of this publication may be reproduced or transmitted by any means, electronic, mechanical, photocopying or otherwise, without the prior permission of the publisher.

This is a work of fiction. Names, characters, businesses, places, events and incidents are either the products of the author's imagination or used in a fictitious manner. Any resemblance to actual persons, living or dead, or actual events is purely coincidental.

Follow on Twitter: @evelyn_winters
www.evelynwinters.co.uk

Other Children's books by Evelyn

Mary Draper Dreams of Castles in the Sky
A Very Giant Tale
An Imp Called Boo
The Why Word
The Blessington Dolls

All these books are available in audio, paperback and Kindle.

Dedicated to Caiden.

Editor: Robin Chambers

Illustrator: Rizal Nugroho

A tale from the heart of Chester...

The Little Big Clockmaker

Once upon a time, many years ago when clocks ticked much louder, there lived a talented clockmaker in an enchanted walled city in the northwest of England. The elf-like man was a master craftsman with an exceptional gift. He had served many a crowned head, but his latest assignment was to be his greatest. Egan Bagley was to create one of the most magnificent clocks the country had ever set eyes on.

    The third Duke of Meadowsville had ordered the clocksmith to create something spectacular: to make the city look more beautiful. For a hundred days and a hundred nights, Egan shut himself away in his dusty workshop, leaving no window uncovered and no door unlocked as he carried out his top-secret work.

One hot night, while tapping, hammering, carving and crafting one of the four intricate faces of the massive clock, he became exhausted. The heat made him feel weak, but he couldn't stop. He feared he would not meet his deadline, and failed to notice a shrunken woman with twisted fingers suddenly standing behind him and clutching a tattered bag. She exhaled - a drawn out rasping sound - which stopped him in his tracks. He spun, nearly losing his balance on his old rickety ladder, and his brass tweezers tinkled to the ground.

"You shouldn't be in here!" he complained.

The peculiar visitor simply observed him and held out her shabby bag. Flummoxed by her presence, Egan raised his eyebrows, peering over his large round glasses. He was sure he had locked his door.

"What do you want?" he snapped.

"Buy a bead from a gypsy, sir?" she

finally asked. Her gravelly voice grated in the workshop's dry air.

Egan sighed in relief and hurried down his ladder. "Yes, yes, if I must," he grabbed a coin and tossed it to the old woman who caught it as if by instinct. She rooted in her bag and brought out a speckled red bead.

"Keep this safe and your gift as a clockmaker will become... extraordinary." She placed it on his palm and closed his hand around it. He would never forget that moment. Her hands were unnaturally cold in the sweltering heat of the night.

Having no idea what she could have meant, he took the bead over to his bench and placed it securely in his tin of tools. He turned to thank her but she'd gone as fast as she'd come. He rushed to the door which was closed and locked. Thinking he'd been hallucinating, he dashed back over to the tin. The bead twinkled wondrously in the light of the worktop lantern.

Days later, he finished the clock's mechanism and carefully pieced the parts together. He wound the handle of the giant clock and proudly listened to its noisy tick. It looked wonderful. He had never made anything so spectacular. All he had to do was paint it...

But time was ticking. He ran up the ladders and removed all four clock-face hands for painting. The deadline was today and he felt anxious the Duke would send someone to find him.

All that day he did not stop, and into the night, and the following day and all the following night... Finally the work of genius towered before him in its full splendour. With all its hands securely back on its faces and with its glorious red and gold detail, incredible ironwork and prominent green copper ogee copula, it surpassed anything the little gnome of a man had ever done or seen before.

And not a moment too soon... There was a thunderous knock on his door: the knock he'd been dreading. He had missed the deadline and feared the wrath of the Duke.

He unlocked and pulled open the heavy door to see the great man standing there with two of his guards. The silken-suited lord rushed past, eager to see his timepiece. He stopped and stared for some time, while Egan waited with baited breath…

"EGAN BAGLEY!" he finally bellowed.

Egan flinched. "Y-Y-Yes," he stammered.

"It's…" the third duke wavered, drawing his eyes away from the clock and resting them on Egan. "It's PERFECT! This IS the Eastgate Clock! Just what the city needs. It will catch the eye of the tourists! It will cause unrest amongst the residents."

He grabbed the clockmaker's hand and shook it furiously. "It is garish, almost shocking; but OUTSTANDING man. Well done!"

Egan wasn't sure if that was good or

bad; but the Duke seemed happy. "I'm sorry for missing the deadline," he said in a rush, "but you see, I had to ensure the quality and detail were just right....."

"What are you talking about?" the Duke cut in. "You are on time. To be perfectly honest I didn't expect you to have such a magnificent piece of work completed on schedule."

"What day is it?" Egan asked.

"Friday; it's Friday, my dear fellow," laughed the Duke.

"Forgive me sir, I thought it was Sunday. I must have lost track of time..."

That night, alone and confused, the clockmaker stared at the four faces above him. He was sure of the days. He'd bought a paper that morning and the date was there clear as day, held tightly in his blistered hand: SUNDAY...

Like a man possessed, he threw the paper down, sprang from the crate he sat on and ran up each of the wooden ladders in turn. One by one he removed the blackened hands and placed them in his tool box next to the shrunken woman's speckled red bead. Then he went home to sleep.

Any reasonable person might be forgiven for thinking he was losing his mind, but Egan Bagley considered it a stroke of genius. Surely no-one else could have come to such a conclusion...

There was a chance, just the merest possibility, that his talents as a clockmaker were now so exceptional that he had - probably, possibly or perhaps even maybe - STOPPED TIME!

Everything appeared normal. Life went on, but when he returned the clock hands to the four faces it became Friday again. He opened his tin of tools and the bewitched bead winked at him. He thought about discarding it but temptation stopped him. There were a few things he could try before throwing it away. With the clock hands safely packed away in the tin, he set off home.

The next day he passed the city's racecourse and watched thoughtfully from the city walls. It was race day, and he had an idea. He would get the names of all the winners, return to the workshop the next day and replace all the clock hands so the day would revert to Friday. Then he would place several bets at the local bookmakers.

As before, the day returned to Friday. He did not see it happen, he did not feel it happen, and he did not know how it could have happened...

But it just did.

He placed a small bet on each of the winning horses, rushed back to the workshop and took off the hands of the clock once more, placing them away in their usual place. The following afternoon he checked the results and returned to the bookmakers to pick up his winnings.

It had worked! He could hardly believe it.

Egan went back to the bookmakers. This time he placed all his winnings on the same winning horses. He was about to make himself one of the richest men in the city. "Just one more bet..." he told himself, and then he would throw the winking bead away.

This time he collected an absolute fortune and attracted a good deal of attention; but as soon as he repositioned the hands on the clock everybody promptly forgot about it. Back in the workshop he remembered his dreams - the ones he'd had when he worked the livelong days - of silken suits and a splendid house, and travelling the world in exclusive luxury, the envy of one and all.

That was what he was going to do, starting tomorrow. Greed had got the better of him, you see, and he placed more bets and went on placing bets until he had... MILLIONS!

He purchased a much sought-after home by the river and spent money like water. He frittered away thousands on the finest clothes. He had servants, overflowing fountains and everything he could ever want. His wealth became renowned.

No-one could fathom how a humble clockmaker could be so well-off...

Of course it didn't stop there. For his own amusement, he entered and won many local competitions. There was no real competition in the longest beard contest, especially when he meddled with time like he did, but he also swept the board in the general knowledge quizzes in all the local pubs. His knowledge on a whole host of topics appeared comprehensive and accurate. He soon acquired the nickname 'Professor Rich'.

People would stop him in the street and ask: "How do you know everything?" and then "Can you spare some change?" Strangely, he never gave them anything. Not one penny...

Spoiled by all that fortune and fame, Egan forgot all about his original plan to dispose of the bead and return to his old life. He went on a Grand Tour of the whole world, living like a king the entire time...

But a day came when he replaced the hands on the clock as he had so many times before, and caught a glimpse of himself in a mirror. He beheld a person he did not recognise. He had aged. His face was wrinkled like an old paper bag and his hair grey as smoke. He had shrunk, just like the old woman, and his hands were gnarled and twisted.

It did not take a genius to work out that time had stopped for everyone but himself.

He felt so distraught he took the bead and threw it in the river. Ashamed of his selfishness, he began to help the people who needed his wealth more than he did. To try and put things right, he began leaving parcels of money for the homeless and needy to find.

Nobody knew who the mysterious angel was until quite by chance a little boy saw a bent old man leaving his sick mother one of the now recognisable parcels of wealth. "It's Professor Rich!"

the boy yelled for the whole neighbourhood to hear. "He's the one who's been leaving all the money for the poor!"

Now it was all gone. The little boy's mother had had the last parcel. But the news of his outstanding generosity spread, and the little clockmaker became a local celebrity – this time for all the right reasons.

He knew he had to return the clock hands to where they belonged one last time: to take everyone back to a time and a place where "Professor Rich" had never existed and he was what he had always been: Egan Bagley, clockmaker extraordinaire.

In the fullness of time, the Eastgate Clock was mounted in its rightful place above the Eastgate walls of Chester, where it has sat ever since. Rumour has it that on very rare occasions, the hands on one or more of its faces momentarily and mysteriously... disappear.

The End

Some Facts

EASTGATE CLOCK

In 1899 the Eastgate Clock was added to the gateway in Chester to commemorate the diamond jubilee of Queen Victoria two years earlier. The clock was actually designed by John Douglas. The clock mechanism was made in 1897 and was wound by a technician each week until it was replaced by an electric mechanism in 1992. It's four faces were glazed by the city council in 1988 after souvenir hunters stole the hands of the clock.

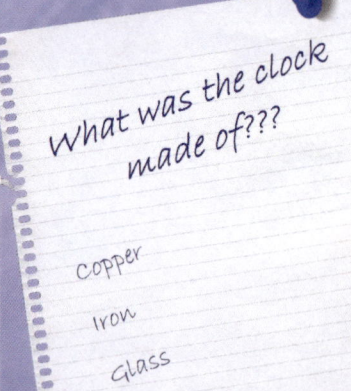

What was the clock made of???

Copper

Iron

Glass

The Eastgate Clock was placed on the gateway in 1899

The inscription on the west side of the clock reads:

"Antiqui colant antiquum dierum: B.C. Roberts, Mayor 1897; J.C. holmes, Mayor 1898"

The inscription on the north side of the clock reads:

"Erected by public subscription & completed A.D. 1899 H. Stolteforth Mayor"

The inscription on the south side of the clock reads:

"This clock was erected by Edward Evans-Lloyd Citizen and Freeman 1897"

The inscription on the east side of the clock reads:

"This clock tower was erected in commemoration of the 60th year of the reign of Victoria, queen and empress",

Eastgate Clock Photograph supplied by local photographer Paul Smith

This book is also available on Kindle and in Audio format.
Narrated by Guy Veryzer.
Visit www.amazon.co.uk

Follow on Twitter: @evelyn_winters
Website: www.evelynwinters.co.uk

The Little Big Clockmaker
Copyright © 2015 by Evelyn Winters

Thank you for reading my story. I would love honest feedback about this book. Your views not only impact other reader's purchasing decisions but your opinion matters to me so I can write more of what you want.

You can leave a review by typing 'A Very Giant Tale' in the Amazon search box.

Please visit www.evelynwinters.co.uk to sign up for my newsletter.

Thank you

Evelyn Winters

Printed in Great Britain
by Amazon